W9-BYB-549

THE ADVENTURES OF MARSHALL & ART

Stranger Danger

by Noel Gyro Potter
illustrated by Joseph Cannon

magic wagon

visit us at www.abdopublishing.com

Dedicated to all of the children in the world...may you always remain safe and protected from harm with a childhood filled with love, laughter and joy.—NGP

Published by Magic Wagon, a division of the ABDO Group, 8000 West 78th Street, Edina, Minnesota 55439. Copyright © 2010 by Abdo Consulting Group, Inc. International copyrights reserved in all countries. All rights reserved. No part of this book may be reproduced in any form without written permission from the publisher.

Looking Glass Library™ is a trademark and logo of Magic Wagon.

Printed in the United States of America, North Mankato, Minnesota.
102009
012010

♻ PRINTED ON RECYCLED PAPER

Text by Noel Gyro Potter
Illustrated by Joseph Cannon
Edited by Stephanie Hedlund and Rochelle Baltzer
Cover and interior design by Neil Klinepier

Library of Congress Cataloging-in-Publication Data
Potter, Noel Gyro.
  Stranger danger / by Noel Gyro Potter ; illustrated by Joseph Cannon.
    p. cm. -- (The adventures of Marshall & Art)
  ISBN 978-1-60270-738-2
  [1. Safety--Fiction. 2. Strangers--Fiction. 3. Brothers--Fiction.] I.
Cannon, Joseph, 1958- ill. II. Title.
  PZ7.P8553St 2010
  [Fic]--dc22
                    2009033968

Ding-dong! Marshall looked through the peephole before opening the door. On the other side, he saw Donovan and Dominick, the twins who lived around the corner.

"Hi, guys! We're playing video games! Wanna play?" Marshall asked.

"Sure," Donovan answered. "What game are you playing?"

"Daredevil Demolition Derby Drivers!" said Marshall. "It's one of our favorites!"

"We've never played that game before," admitted Dominick.

"It's fun! We'll help you," Art said.

The hour passed so fast that it seemed like five minutes. Marshall and Art's mom, Marti, reminded Donovan and Dominick that it was time for them to head home. The boys only had a short walk, but they had promised their mom they would be home before dark.

"Thanks for having us, Mrs. James!" Dominick hollered.

"You're welcome," Marti said. "Marshall, Art, why don't you walk with the boys until they get just around the corner."

"Okay, we'll be right back!" said Art.

Marshall, Art, Donovan, and Dominick talked and laughed as they passed the first few houses. Then, a car suddenly appeared out of nowhere. It stopped right alongside the four boys. The window began to roll down and a man behind the wheel called out to the boys. They stopped on the sidewalk for only a moment.

"Hey, kids, I noticed someone following you! Get into my car quick and I'll take you all home so we can call the sheriff. Hurry!" the man said.

The boys had never seen this man before. Donovan and Dominick were so frightened, they could hardly move. Luckily, Marshall and Art recognized the trick that this stranger was using. It was one of the very tricks that their parents had warned them about!

"Everybody run to our house!" Marshall yelled.

All four boys turned and ran as fast they could. Art knew the stranger's car couldn't turn around as fast them.

Then, Marshall and Art began to scream as loudly as they could, "FIRE, FIRE, FIRE!" They yelled until they safely reached their house.

It worked! The stranger took off down the street!

Marshall and Art's dad, Johnny, heard the shouting and ran out of the house. Other neighbors also opened their doors to see what the yelling was all about.

"What's going on? Are you all right?" Johnny asked worriedly.

Art was out of breath, but he spoke up first, "Dad, a stranger pulled up alongside us when we were walking Donovan and Dominick home! He tried to trick us by saying that someone was following us and that we should get in his car to be safe!"

Marshall tried to catch his breath, too. Finally, he said, "Dad, it was just like the trick you told us about. He said he was going to help us!"

"Boys, get inside! We need to call the sheriff and make a report before he tries his tricks on some other children who might actually believe him!" urged Johnny.

When Sheriff Katz and Sheriff Davis arrived, the boys gave the officers useful details about the stranger and his car.

"You boys did the right things," said Sheriff Katz. "The longer kids stand around and talk to strangers, the more chance the stranger has of using their tricks on them. It's better to get away as fast as you can, just like you did. Only when it's a real emergency, such as this, yelling 'fire' is a smart way to get everyone's attention."

19

Johnny and Marti called Donovan and Dominick's mom, Carmen, to let her know what had happened and that the boys were safe. Carmen arrived minutes later and hugged her sons tightly. Donovan and Dominick excitedly told her how Marshall and Art's fast thinking and stranger danger knowledge saved them from the stranger and his sneaky tricks.

"I never thought something like this could happen in our neighborhood. I was very wrong," Carmen said.

"Strangers try their tricks on kids everywhere, every day," Johnny said. "That's why children need to be taught about these tricks. The more kids know what to look out for, the safer they'll be."

"I'm glad you taught us that a stranger is anyone we don't know! You said even if they try to convince us that they're going to help us, don't trust someone you don't know," said Marshall to his dad. Art added, "I never thought I could run as fast as I did today!"

26

Donovan asked, "But, couldn't Marshall and Art have used karate to get away?"

Johnny answered quickly, "Even an experienced black belt should never choose to fight if there is a way to escape. The farther you are from a stranger, the safer you'll be!"

"Yeah, tonight our best weapons were definitely our feet!" said Art.

"No, Art. I think our best weapons were those black belt brains that you and Marshall used tonight! Maybe, you could teach us some more safety tips," said Donovan.

"That's a great idea! I have a feeling there is a lot more to learn from this family besides video games. Good night and thank you for everything," Carmen said as she, Donovan, and Dominick headed out the door.

As the James family sat down to dinner, they all gave thanks for the stranger danger knowledge that had kept Marshall and Art and their friends safe. They decided to start teaching Harley everything they knew about strangers to keep him safe, too.

Stranger Danger Tips

Marshall and Art used their stranger danger knowledge to stay safe Here are some stranger safety tips to remember:

Children:
- Anyone you don't know is a stranger! Strangers can be teenagers or adults.
- Adults shouldn't approach kids for directions or for help. Strangers who intend to harm you will try to confuse you or be too friendly. Do not listen to *anything* a stranger says and never let a stranger get close to you!
- A knock on the door and a stranger saying "My dog ran in your backyard. Can I go get him?" or "I'm an undercover police officer. Come with me quickly!" are just two of the ways strangers try to get kids. Don't believe them!
- If a stranger approaches you or appears out of nowhere, immediately run in the opposite direction and yell, "FIRE! FIRE! FIRE!" because it will get immediate attention.

Adults:
- Never permit a young child to answer the door. Children have a false sense of security and usually open the door believing it's okay because an adult is there. However, a child can be abducted simply by opening a door.
- Child predators often locate homes where it is obvious that children live. Bikes and skateboards in the street or toys in the front yard easily let strangers know that children can be found in the home.
- Children are no match for adult ingenuity, but you can make them aware so they know what to do when a stranger appears. Be proactive and do all that you can to inform and protect them.